ME and the BAD GUYS

ME
and the
BAD GUYS

by
Shirley Gordon

Pictures by
Edward Frascino

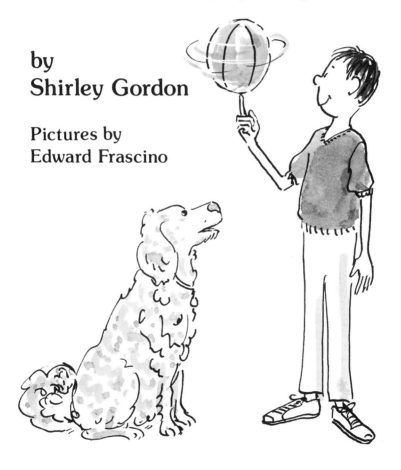

Harper & Row, Publishers

Library of Congress Cataloging in Publication Data
Gordon, Shirley.
    Me and the bad guys.

    SUMMARY: When a series of small frustrations at school causes Mike Berger to lose his temper, he discovers you can't always tell the good guys from the bad guys.
    [1. School stories.   2. Behavior—Fiction]
    I. Frascino, Edward.   II. Title.
    PZ7.G6594Me   [Fic]   79-9611
    ISBN 0-06-022116-X
    ISBN 0-06-022117-8 (lib. bdg.)

To
Jennifer and Frank Hughes
and
"Mrs. Mickey Mouse"

CONTENTS

AN EXTRA PAIR OF EARS

It's just like I always hear my mom say. The trouble with this world is there's no justice.

That's why I have this thing about Walt Disney. I want him to come back and take charge of *everything.* Things would be a lot better then, let me tell you!

But I can't explain this to anybody. I tried to once, and that was my big mistake. There are some things you can't talk about, even to your best friend. . . .

During recess one day, we're all sitting around on our favorite bench under the pepper tree, the only green and shady spot on the playground. Greg, who most of the time I think

1

of as my best friend, blurts out, "D'you know what Mike's waiting for? He's waiting for Walt Disney to defrost."

"Huh?" Ron scowls. Ron is no best friend of mine. In fact, he's almost the worst.

"When Disney died, they say he had his body frozen," Greg goes on, "so if they find the cure for what killed him, he can be brought back to life."

"*Eee-oooh—how gross!*" squeals Linda, this girl whose legs are about as long and skinny and pink as a flamingo's.

Girls always hang around us because Greg is absolutely the most good-looking guy in the entire school. He looks like a surfer with his tanned face and blond hair and blue eyes, but the truth is he doesn't even ride a skateboard.

I look like just what I am—the basketball type, tall with big hands and big feet.

"What does Mike want with Walt Disney?" asks Nicole, this ballet-type girl who butts into our business all the time. I keep stepping on her ballet toes with my big basketball feet because she's always got them stuck in my way.

Greg shrugs. "Mike's just a Mickey Mouse freak, that's all."

It's true. I have a big Mickey Mouse poster up on the wall of my room, and a little plastic statue of Mickey on my bookshelf. And I have

this book that tells all about how Walt Disney first invented Mickey Mouse about fifty years ago.

The way I feel about Mickey is the way Mr. Disney writes about him in this book: "Mickey is a pretty nice fellow who never does anybody any harm, who gets into scrapes through no fault of his own, but always manages to come up grinning. You just can't help liking Mickey."

You sure can't! Mickey's a real hero. Anyway, he's *my* hero.

I explained about Mickey to Greg once, but he didn't understand one bit or he wouldn't be blabbing my business all over the place now. Some best friend!

"Mikey the Mouseketeer—how cute!" gurgles Nicole.

"Shut up!"

"When you gonna grow up, Berger?" Ron sneers.

"Get lost!"

"Better lay off," Greg puts in, "or he'll have Mickey Mouse sick Pluto on you."

"Some pal you are," I remind Greg.

Finally, Nicole reaches over and messes up my hair—which is something that really bugs me. "Aw, let's not pick on little *Mikey* Mouse anymore," she baby talks.

Lucky for her, just then the bell rings and we have to go back into class, or I might step on one of her ballet toes on purpose.

But a couple days later, in American History, I'm sitting at my desk paying attention to my own business when suddenly somebody plops something on my head.

I know without turning around it's Nicole because she sits at the desk right behind me, which is not very relaxing. I always know she's there, because she leans forward and breathes down my neck a lot (she smells like a stick of spearmint gum), and I'm always afraid she's going to make a grab for my hair.

Now, I guess right away what she's put on my head—a pair of Mouseketeer ears. Very funny.

All these giggles start bouncing around the room. Mr. Rosenbloom probably hears them, but so far he still has his face down, reading some papers on his desk, with just the top of his bald head showing.

I want to reach up and whisk off the ears and shove them away in my desk before Old Rosie looks up and sees them. But if I do, I'll be chicken.

Which is worse—being a chicken or a mouse?

It's too late. Old Rosie looks up, fastens his

fish eye on me, and makes a general announcement: "It is not permitted to wear a hat—of any nature—in the classroom."

I feel my ears—my *real* ears—turn red.

"Mr. Berger." Mr. Rosenbloom always addresses us formally like that, as if we were already grown up. Usually it makes me feel good, but not this time. "Mr. Berger, I must ask you to remove whatever that is you have on your head, and bring it up to my desk."

"Yes, sir." (*Snicker-snicker* behind me.)

I reach up and take off the Mouseketeer ears—I'm glad of that, at least—and start The Long Walk up to Old Rosie's desk at the front of the room. I can feel all these eyes boring holes into the back of my neck, and it gets as red as my ears.

By the time I make it to the front of the room, my whole head feels like it's on fire. I hand the ears over to Mr. Rosenbloom and he puts them in his bottom desk drawer, along with his collection of comic books, Frisbees, and transistor radios.

"You may retrieve your possession after class," he decrees, which means I'm only charged with a minor offense. Old Rosie has had Ron's transistor radio in his bottom desk drawer for a whole month.

"Thank you, sir," I answer, and make it back

to my desk as fast as I can. (*Snicker-snicker, smirk-smirk* behind me.)

Boy! Girls get away with murder! All through the rest of American History, I sit there trying to think of some evil spell to cast on all the girls in the world.

Especially Nicole.

SUBTRACT ONE BASKETBALL, AND ADD YOGURT

After American History, I sneak off to my locker to put away those good old Mouseketeer ears to take home. (Only I sure wouldn't want Nicole to know!)

Rats! The lock's dangling loose. My locker's been busted into!

I swing open the door and check inside. Looks like there's only one thing missing. But it happens to be the one thing I can't live without—my basketball.

At recess, I meet the guys outside and tell them what's happened. We stroll over to our bench under the pepper tree to talk about it. Without my basketball, we have nothing better to do.

"I bet I know who it was," Ron says, stretching his whole self out on the bench as if he owned it. Greg sits down and shoves him over from one end and I sit down and shove him over from the other.

If anybody knows who took my ball, it's Ron. He hangs out a lot with the bad kids—I mean, the kids who are always up to something. Ron has this pointy nose that's a perfect fit for his rat personality. He's definitely the snitching type.

"Never mind who took it," I tell him. "I want it back, that's all."

"It was Pete, I betcha." Ron-the-Rat just has to snitch anyway.

"Pete doesn't even like to play basketball," I remind him, giving my lunch sack a shake to see if I can guess what's in it.

Ron grins. "I know. He just likes to steal."

"Then maybe he'll give it back," says Greg, trying to get the idea across. "I mean, what else is he going to do with it?"

"Maybe he will," Ron agrees, thinking about it. "If you don't get him into trouble for it."

"*Stealing* something is supposed to get you into trouble, not giving it back," I point out.

"Just tell him to give the ball back," says Greg, "and we'll get the F.B.I. to drop the case."

I decide to eat my lunch since, without my

basketball, I have nothing else to do. That'll leave me with nothing at all to do during lunch, but I won't worry about that now.

Only when I dig into my lunch sack, there's just a tuna salad sandwich on some kind of dumb health bread and some yogurt in a Tupperware dish that I have to remember to bring home or my mom'll kill me.

"If Pete wanted to steal something out of my locker," I complain to Ron, "why didn't he steal my lunch?"

"He probably saw what it was," says Ron, making a face as I swallow a spoonful of yogurt.

It's even black walnut—my unfavorite flavor. Man, my life is getting to be The Pits lately.

"Look, you guys," Ron says finally. "I'll go check out Pete and see what I can do—okay?"

Greg glares at him, steely-eyed. "Okay."

Ron glances at me, but I don't say anything. I just give him my best Godfather look.

"It's like having to deal with the Mafia around here," I complain to Greg after Ron takes off. "Only right now, I don't know which is worse—the Mafia, or *girls.* Even if he did rip off my basketball, Pete takes second place to Nicole on *my* Ten Most Wanted list."

Greg busts out laughing. "You sure looked stupid, man—with those dumb mouse ears on your head." Sometimes Greg really does forget he's supposed to be my best friend.

While Greg and I are sitting there discussing things, the Safety spots us. Okay—a Safety is around just to keep everybody out of trouble and see that nobody gets hurt, right?

And there isn't any reason for him to bother

two guys who aren't doing anything but sitting there minding their own business, right?

Wrong!

He comes swaggering up to us with this too-friendly smile. "As long as you two musclemen have nothing else to do, I have a job for you. Mr. Saunders needs some help carrying out the extra tables and benches for the Fiesta on Friday."

"But . . ."

"We were going to—"

"It'll earn you some school service points," the Safety reminds us. Somehow, racking up points for school service doesn't appeal to me as much as making points shooting baskets.

The Safety hustles us across the yard to where Mr. Saunders is waiting to put us to work.

"How about this!" mutters Greg. "You and I get caught like a couple of sitting ducks for doing nothing, while Pete gets away scot-free with stealing your basketball."

"What else is new?" I mutter back.

MY PROBLEMS
GET MULTIPLIED

"All right, men—heave ho." Mr. Saunders doesn't move anything but his mouth while Greg and I lug the heavy tables and benches out onto the playground.

I try to look on the bright side. "Anyway, the exercise'll help keep us in shape for the next game—if we ever get my ball back."

"And Friday's the Fiesta," says Greg. "All those good things to eat!"

Whenever we have a school event, some of the mothers knock themselves out making these great pies and cookies and cakes to sell for the P.T.A. After the all-American health-food lunches my mom's been packing for me lately, I'm sure looking forward to eating something that's really bad for me.

14

The only bummer about the Fiesta is that we all have to perform some kind of dance. The group I'm in has to do a square dance called The All-American Promenade.

I wouldn't mind too much if I hadn't gotten stuck with this leftover girl named Lisa as my partner. She's about two feet tall with red hair and freckles, and she doesn't want to dance with me any more than I want to dance with her.

Br-raaa-ang . . . The bell signals recess is over. Greg and I put down the bench we're carrying and tell Mr. Saunders, "We have to get back to our classes now."

He gives us each a pat on the back and says, "Good job, men."

Greg is lucky because his next class is P.E. Mine is Math, and the teacher, Mrs. Patterson, ought to be a drill sergeant in the Marine Corps. When we sit at our desks, she makes us keep our backs as straight as rulers—even when we're trying to figure out a really hard math problem.

It's impossible for me to sit up straight and think at the same time.

After what seems like half a century, the bell clangs again and Math is finally over. I'll probably get a D on today's test (if I'm lucky), plus a minus for hunching over my desk trying to think.

I head for the auditorium next, because it's time to practice the dancing for the Fiesta. Greg is already there. "Hear anything yet about your basketball?" he asks right away.

I shake my head. Ron-the-Rat shows up across the room, but he makes out like he doesn't see us.

Ol' blue-eyed Nicole (she has big round eyes that look like they were drawn on her face with a blue Crayola) is standing over in the corner, giggling with Flamingo-Legs Linda and Sweet-Tooth Sherri, this other girl who always has a Milky Way in her mouth.

16

I squint my eyes and concentrate on putting my evil spell on them, but they keep right on giggling.

Ms. Salisbury, who's in charge of the dancing, claps her hands. "All right, young ladies and gentlemen, find your partners and form your squares."

I look around for my partner. With all the seats folded up against the wall to make room for the dancing, the auditorium looks as big as the Houston Astrodome, and it's hard to find a Munchkin in a crowd—even one with red hair and freckles.

"I can't find my partner," I finally report to Ms. Salisbury.

"Oh, dear!" She flutters her hands like a pair of fans and looks so shook up that I feel sorry I have to bother her with my problem. "I remember now," she explains. "Lisa's asthma has flared up, and her mother doesn't think she should dance."

Hooray! If I don't have a partner, I won't have to dance, either. But the next minute, I feel disappointed. To be honest, square dancing is kind of fun. And to be even more honest, I don't really want to be left out of the program.

Ms. Salisbury flutters on. "Oh, don't worry, Michael—you're still going to be in the program." I guess she can tell what I'm thinking.

She smiles at me with all of her teeth, which she has a lot of. "I shall meet the emergency and dance with you myself."

My mouth drops open, but I don't say anything. I hope Ms. Salisbury can't tell what I'm thinking now!

When she starts do-si-do-ing me around the auditorium, I'd rather be back in Math class, taking the worst exam that Drill Sergeant Patterson ever thought up, or even sitting in front

of Old Rosie with those Mouseketeer ears on my head.

Am I ever going to get razzed about *this*! Especially by you-know-who. Every time I glance over at Crayola-Eyes Nicole, she's practically biting her lips off to keep from laughing. And Ron-the-Rat has his mouth open with his teeth sticking out, giving me the old silent horselaugh.

They're supposed to be keeping their minds

on their feet, but they're too busy watching Ms. Salisbury toss me around like a salad. They don't dare laugh out loud, of course, but they're sure going to let me have it later.

Only I can't worry about that now. I have to concentrate on keeping my big number nine Adidas out of Ms. Salisbury's way. She's wearing some silly sandals with her bare toes sticking out, so I could cripple her for life.

Br-raaa-ang . . . Finally! I feel like a punch-drunk prizefighter at the end of the final round.

Ms. Salisbury lets go of me and flip-flaps in her sandals across the room to turn off the record player. There's a general stampede in the direction of the Exit doors.

Ms. Salisbury claps her hands and hollers over the noise. "Remember! Friday! Boys in their bright-colored shirts, girls in their old-fashioned dresses and petticoats."

Omigosh! I'm going to have to dance in front of the whole school with Ms. Salisbury in her petticoats! I think I'm going to be sick.

GOOD GUYS AND BAD GUYS

For once Greg is all sympathy as we beat it out of the auditorium. "Man, if I were you, I'd pretend to get sick so I could be absent Friday."

I put my hand to my forehead. "I don't think I'll have to pretend."

Nicole is waiting outside, all doubled up, laughing so hard she's probably going to have a heart attack.

I look down my nose at her. "Nothing is that funny."

She can hardly stop laughing long enough to answer back. "You . . . *ha ha* . . .should have . . . *ha* . . . seen . . . *ha ha ha* . . . yourself . . . *ha ha ha ha ha!*"

"You have a really weird sense of humor," I comment, and walk away.

Greg and I go sit on our bench on the playground. Since it's lunch and I've already eaten mine, I'm only interested in collaring Rat-Nosed Ron to see if he's made any progress getting my basketball back.

"If he has," I grumble, "I suppose he's going to claim a reward."

Greg digs into his lunch sack. "You can give him my Twinkies. He'll settle for anything to eat."

So would I. I wish I hadn't eaten my lunch ahead of time. But I stick the Twinkies package in my pocket, in case Ron shows up with my ball.

Greg divvies up his sandwich. "Want half of my ham-and-cheese?"

"Thanks—I'm starved."

"Hey, Twinkletoes!" Too-Tall Tommy, the captain of our basketball team, waves at me like he has a girl's hanky in his hand. "Teacher's dancing darling!"

"Yeah, who does Salisbury think you are— John Travolta?" Billy Saxton snickers. Billy Saxton couldn't sink a basket if he tried, but he's a great snickerer.

All the time we're sitting there, I really get it. I'm not surprised that everybody in school has heard about me having to dance with Ms. Salisbury. Besides her big blue-Crayola eyes, Nicole has a big red-Crayola mouth.

"Yo! Ham-Berger!" Arty hollers from clear across the playground. All the gang call me "Ham-Berger" or "Cheese-Berger" sometimes, but Smarty-Arty *always* does. "How about it, Cheese-Berger—you and ol' lady Salisbury gonna hit the discos tonight?"

"All *right!*" Suddenly Greg gives a cheer and jumps up from the bench.

"ALL RIGHT!"

Ron comes strutting across the playground with my ball, and Greg and I both greet him as if he's some kind of hero—just for bringing back what was mine in the first place.

Only—then I take another look. It's my basketball all right, but it's been mortally wounded. Ron hands it over and I take one feel of it. It's about as round and solid as a marshmallow.

Man, I start to steam inside. "Thanks," I spit the words at Ron through my teeth. "Thanks a lot."

"Pete says it rolled out into the street and a car hit it. It wasn't his fault." Ron gives us this ratty story. "Anyway," he reminds me, "I got it back for you."

I take Greg's Twinkies out of my pocket and hand them over. "Here's your reward. Sorry they're a little squashed." But being sarcastic is a waste where Ron's concerned.

"See you around." He struts off, licking the creme filling out of a squashed Twinkie.

Greg and I try to think of a game to play with a flat basketball, but there isn't any. We could sign out one of the school balls—if they're not all signed out already—but they're too duddy.

"We may as well go ask Mr. Saunders if he has another job for us," Greg says finally.

I make a face. "That's the trouble with us. We think like Good Guys."

"Right," agrees Greg. "If I were Ron, I'd go con somebody else out of *his* Twinkies."

"And if I were Pete, I'd be busy busting into people's lockers and rolling their basketballs out into the street to get run over."

Greg nods. "The Bad Guys have all the fun."

All we can do is sit out the rest of lunch period until the good old bell rings. The only classes I have in the afternoon are Library and P.E., so at least the rest of this day should go okay.

Nobody can bother anybody in Library, because everybody has to be quiet. Especially with Mrs. Pemberton in charge. Mrs. Pemberton is the oldest teacher in the school (she looks like your typical little old lady in the TV commercial who asks Mr. Whipple not to squeeze the toilet paper). And she's really old-fashioned about things like being quiet in a library.

Some kids can't stand it quiet, so they sneak in their pocket transistors and sit there with the earplugs in their ears. Mrs. Pemberton doesn't seem to notice. Or if she does, she must think half the kids in school wear hearing aids.

I find an empty table in the corner away from everybody, and break out my science book to study a boring geological time chart for a test we have coming up. Then two guys with earplugs in their ears come and sit at the table beside me.

I don't know them but I've seen Ron-the-Rat with them a couple of times, so they probably mean trouble. I could get up and move, but I have my books and papers spread out all over the place.

And besides, I was here first. Why should I let a couple of other guys take over?

One of them takes the earplug out of his ear and tries to stick it into mine. I jerk my head away, but he grins and tries it again. "Cut it out!" I mumble under my breath.

Mrs. Pemberton stares over her glasses at us. I slide down in my chair and bury my face in my book. But this guy doesn't give up. He keeps trying to stick the plug in my ear.

"Bug off!" I mutter. Mrs. Pemberton gives me a sharp look, and the two guys snicker at each other. Right about now, I'd like to knock their heads together.

But as soon as Mrs. Pemberton turns away, I get the earplug jammed in my ear again. "LEAVE ME ALONE!" I *holler—right out loud* in the library!

As soon as I hear myself, I wish I could dive under the table. About fifty pairs of eyes stare at me, and Mrs. Pemberton hotfoots it over. By now the two guys have their transistors and earplugs stashed out of sight and their heads bent over their notebooks, like a pair of angels.

Mrs. Pemberton stands over me like a thundercloud. "Michael," she hisses in her library whisper, "I shall have to ask you to leave the library and report immediately to the principal's office."

I feel my face turn beet-red. I'm not embarrassed—I'm *mad*!

Not just mad. STEAMED!

A BUMPER STICKER

I've never been sent down to the principal's office for anything serious before. (I'm one of the Good Guys, remember.)

Mrs. Dunbar, who works in the outside office, is surprised to see me. "Why, Michael— aren't you supposed to be in Library this period?" Mrs. Dunbar knows every kid in school and where he's supposed to be every minute.

"Mrs. Pemberton said I should come down here." I don't feel like talking much because I'm too mad, so I hope she doesn't ask me anything else.

She doesn't get the chance to, because just then Mr. Mankowitz, the principal, comes into the office. "Well, young man, are you here to see me?"

"Yes, sir."

"Come in, then." I follow him into the other room and wait while he frowns over some papers on his desk, with this mean look on his face. I almost forget about being mad, because now I'm scared.

Finally Mr. Mankowitz sits down at his desk and waves at the chair across from it. "Sit down, sit down."

I sit on the edge of the chair.

"What's your name?"

"Berger. Michael Berger."

"Well then, Berger . . . what's your problem?" He glares at me, and I notice he only has one eyebrow that goes all the way across his forehead. No wonder he looks so mean.

"Mrs. Pemberton sent me down, because I yelled out loud in the library."

"Yelled? *Out loud?* In the *library*!" Mr. Mankowitz makes it sound like a federal offense. "What was it you had to say, young man, that was so important you had to yell it out loud in the library?"

"I'M MAD AS HELL AND I'M NOT GOING TO TAKE IT ANYMORE!"

Wow! I'm sure surprised when *that* comes out of me. And Mr. Mankowitz's one eyebrow slides right up to the top of his head!

It's something I saw on a bumper sticker

once, and it's how I feel, all right. But I sure
wasn't planning to yell it in Mr. Mankowitz's
face.

He settles back in his chair, frowning. "Well,
Berger—it seems you do have a problem."

"Yes, sir."

"We'll have to see what we can do about it,
won't we?"

"Yes, sir."

31

He picks up a pen and writes something on a piece of paper. "I'm going to send a note home to your mother."

Oh, no!

Mr. Mankowitz looks up from his desk. "You may go back to your classes now."

"Yes, sir."

When I stand up, my knees feel rubbery. And when I walk to the door, it feels like I'm wearing snowshoes. I open the door and walk through the outside office. Mrs. Dunbar has her head inside a file cabinet, so I make it all the way out into the hall without her noticing me.

That's lucky, because if she'd said anything to me—who knows? I might have yelled in *her* face, too.

According to the clock in the hall, it's almost time for Library to be over, so there's no point going back up there. Besides, Mrs. Pemberton probably wouldn't let me back in.

It seems funny to be all alone in the empty hall. It's super quiet. I look at all the dusty footprints on the floor. I bet I could figure out all the different brands of sneakers just by the treadmarks.

Thinking about all the other kids at their desks in their classrooms, I wish I was still at the table in the corner of the library studying my science book. If only those guys hadn't come around . . . if only they'd left me alone. . . .

Man, things are sure piling up on me! What next? When I get to P.E., I'll probably find out somebody's busted into my gym locker and stolen my sweats, and then the coach will read *me* out because I'm not suited up.

As I head for the door, the sound of my footsteps in the empty hall bounces off the walls. With this great echo and the mood I'm in, I can't help myself. When I get to the end of the hall, I put my hands to my mouth and yell one more time.

"I'M MAD AS HELL AND I'M NOT GOING TO TAKE IT ANYMORE!"

The words ricochet down the hall and back. I beat it outside and run like crazy. Only instead of going into the gym I keep on running, over to the athletic field and out onto the track. I run around and around it, faster and faster, one lap after another.

Sweat pours off me, and I'm breathing so hard I sound like I'm crying. Then I realize— I *am* crying!

Jeez! Maybe Mr. Mankowitz is right. Maybe I *do* have a problem.

THE LIE

As soon as I realize I'm crying, I stop. I pull off the track and lean against the rail, panting like a thirsty puppy. I rub my fist across my face and feel the tears.

Man, I have to get myself together before P.E. I take a big deep breath and slowly let it out. Then I walk into the john and stick my face under the faucet.

The cold water helps. My mom says everybody needs a good cry once in a while. Maybe she's right. I don't think I've cried since I was about two years old.

But I don't want anybody to see me! I yank out a paper towel, wipe off my face, and get my comb out of my back pocket. Combing my hair always makes me feel better.

Only—in the mirror where I expect to see one face, I see two! And this other fat face is giving me a big smirk. I turn around and come eyeball-to-eyeball with Boom-Boom Bradley. Boom-Boom plays the bass drum in the school band, and speaking of Bad Guys, he should be in *The Guinness Book of World Records.*

"How long you been in here?" I want to know.

He curls his lip. "What's it to you, Crybaby?"

That answers my question. "I wasn't cryin', I was sweatin'. I just ran about fifty laps."

"Yeah, sure."

"Listen, Bradley—if you try to make something out of this, I'll—"

"You'll *what*?"

I think about it. Boom-Boom Bradley is about two times my size, in every direction. And he's worked up a lot of muscles carrying that bass drum around. I decide to keep things vague.

"Never mind. Just don't, that's all." I turn and walk out of the john, just as the bell rings. I head for my locker to get suited up.

P.E. turns out to be just what I need. Nothing sounds better than the squeak of sneakers on the freshly waxed gym floor. And the first thing the coach does is toss a basketball at me—a real *live* basketball!

"All right, Berger—let's see you drop one in."

The other guys make way and watch me dribble the ball across the floor and flick it into the basket like it's what I was born to do.

The coach slaps his hands together. "Beautiful!"

He has us practice lay-ups and passing and shooting, and I forget everything that's been happening to me lately. When I'm shooting baskets, I can't think of anything else.

But after P.E., when I get dressed and come out of the gym, Nicole is there with her big starey blue eyes. Boom-Boom Bradley has already done his dirty work.

"What's the matter, *Mikey* Mouse?" Nicole baby talks again. "Somebody step on your tail and make you cry?" She sounds as if she's just trying to bug me, like always. But it's funny— her face has a wrinkled-up worried look, like she really wants to know if something's wrong.

Only I don't care anymore.

"Mind your own business," I snap at her as I flag down Greg across the playground and head over to him. Nicole tags along.

"Hey, what happened?" Greg asks right away. "I heard you got sent down from the library."

"Is that why you were crying in the bathroom?" Nicole goes right on sticking her dumb pug nose into my business.

"Crying?" Greg stares at me with his mouth open.

"I wasn't crying, I was sweating."

"Not according to Boom-Boom Bradley." Nicole doesn't give up. "He swears you were crying."

"Big-mouth Bradley doesn't know what he's talking about."

"You better not let him hear you say that."

"I don't care if he does."

"What were you crying about?" asks Greg. How about that? My best friend!

I turn on him. "You mean you believe that louse Bradley instead of me?"

"I didn't say that."

"Anyway, whatever I do is my own business," I yell at both of them and walk away.

"Hey, wait up!" Greg runs after me. "I didn't mean I believe Bradley instead of you. I just wanted to know if there's something wrong, that's all."

"Nothing's wrong," I tell him.

"You sure?" He takes hold of my shoulder and swings me around to face him. "Honest, Mike—were you crying in the john?"

I jerk away from him. "Leave me alone!"

I take off, and this time Greg doesn't try to stop me. "I'll talk to you later—okay?" he calls after me.

I don't answer. It seems to me your best friend ought to believe *you*, not your enemy— even if you're the one who's lying.

THE LETTER

Usually, walking home from school is one of my favorite times of the day. I walk along this busy street where you always see things like cops giving guys tickets, old ladies jogging, and stray cats and dogs running all over the place.

Once, a motorcycle wedding went by—the groom in his tuxedo was riding on this big orange Honda and the bride was hanging on in back with her white wedding dress and veil blowing in the wind.

But today's the day my mom's probably going to get Mr. Mankowitz's letter in the mail, so that's all I can think about. I jaywalk across the street in the middle of the block and dare a cop to give me a ticket.

Mom's still at work at the art gallery when I get home from school. I always get this funny feeling as I walk into the house and nobody's there—just the furniture and lamps and pictures and things in all this *quiet*. It feels like the whole world has stopped.

And there it is! A long white envelope on the

floor under the mail slot. It's addressed to my mom and it's from the school, all right.

I pick it up and hold it in the light, but I can't see anything. I could steam it open, but what good would that do? I'll find out what it says soon enough.

My dog Jumbo is scratching the back door to pieces for me to let him in. I put down the envelope and open the door. Jumbo jumps all over me. He's just the kind of company I need. I don't ever have to explain anything to Jumbo.

"Do I, fella!"

He smiles and wags his tail.

In the kitchen I get a handful of Oreos and a couple of dog biscuits, and Jumbo follows me into my room. I toss my book bag down on my bed and look around at all my *Star Wars* and Mickey Mouse junk. It feels good, being safe in my room with all my things—with the little statue of Mickey standing guard on my bookshelf.

"It's almost time for the Mouseketeers," I remind Jumbo. "That's what I need—some good Disney magic."

I turn on the TV and put on my new Mouseketeer ears. Jumbo barks at me.

"It's all right, Jumbo," I squeak in a high funny cartoon voice. "I'm Mickey Mouse. I'm a Good Guy."

43

Jumbo stops barking and cocks his head at me. "And you're Pluto," I tell him. "C'mon—let's join the Mouseketeers, Pluto!"

The program comes on, and I stretch out on top of my bed, on my soft warm *Star Wars* comforter, with Pluto beside me. "M - i - c - k - e - y M - o - u - s - e . . ." I sing along with the Mouseketeers.

I wish I could be a real Mouseketeer, smiling and singing and tap-dancing on TV. . . .

I bet Pete and Boom-Boom and those guys wouldn't bother me then. . . .

Nicole and her dumb girl friends would want my autograph, and maybe I'd give it to them and maybe I wouldn't. . . .

One of my favorite cartoons comes on, and

Donald Duck struts across the screen. "Hi, Donald!" I call out in my Mickey Mouse voice.

"Hello, Mickey!" he quacks back at me.

"C'mon, Pluto," I holler. "Let's go to the Magic Kingdom!"

We get there just in time! The pirate ship is coming around the bend, a black skull-and-crossbones flag flying from its tall mast. It's Peg-Leg Pete and the Pirates!

BOOM! BOOM! The cannons spit fire from the deck of the big ship.

Mickey and Pluto run along Main Street, past all the little gingerbread houses and shops, spreading the alarm through the Kingdom. "Hurry, everybody! They're trying to destroy the magic castle!" shouts Mickey. "We'll shoot off the fireworks to scare the pirates away!"

Sssssss—POW! go the skyrockets, bursting into color high above the towers of the magic castle.

"Look, Pluto—it's Tinkerbell!" Mickey smiles up at the tiny fairy figure flying across the sky on silvery wings, waving her sparkling magic wand.

"Arf! Arf! Arf!" barks Pluto.

"The Magic Kingdom is saved!" cheers Mickey.

"Arf! Arf!"

No, it's not Pluto barking—it's Jumbo. He's not barking at Tinkerbell. He's barking at Mom, coming in the front door.

I take off my Mouseketeer ears and turn off the TV. "See you later, Mickey," I say in a quiet voice. I'm not in the Magic Kingdom anymore. I'm in my room. And my mom's home.

Probably reading Mr. Mankowitz's letter!

PETTICOATS . . .

All the time I was worried about what the letter from Mr. Mankowitz was going to say, I'd thought of all kinds of things. But I never thought it would say I was *crazy*!

"Mike—what's all this about?" Mom asks. "Mr. Mankowitz says he's making an appointment for you with the school psychologist."

I explain to Mom what happened.

"If all that happened to me, I'd feel like yelling too," she says. "Only it's too bad you did it in the principal's office." *She* doesn't think I'm crazy.

"I know." I forget to tell her that I yelled up and down the hall, too.

There's one other thing I don't tell her about,

either—on purpose. That crying-in-the-john business. Even though she believes in crying, she'd probably make a big deal about it, like Greg.

Then she says, "Maybe Mr. Mankowitz has a good idea, Mike. Maybe you'd feel better if you did have a talk with the school psychologist."

"But I'm not crazy."

"It doesn't mean you're crazy. He's there to help kids with their problems."

Great. I wonder if he can help a kid with his problem if the kid doesn't know what his problem is.

Only the next morning I know what my problem is—it's Fiesta day, and I have to dance with Ms. Salisbury! When I take off for school, Greg is waiting at the corner to walk the rest of the way with me.

"Hi, Mike—you okay?"

"I'm fine."

He has on a bright red shirt and I'm wearing a bright green one. "We look like a stop-and-go signal," he says, trying to get a laugh out of me.

I don't think it's that funny.

But when we get to school and I get a look at the girls in their weird dresses and petticoats, I crack up. Now, *that's* funny!

Nicole stomps across the playground. "What d'you think you're laughing at?"

"You," I tell her. "You look like something out of the Civil War."

"I bet you won't think it's so funny when you see *your* partner," she sniffs.

I take a nervous look around. "Have you seen Ms. Salisbury? What's she got on?"

"You'll see." Nicole smirks, and flounces away in her funny ruffles.

"Hey, Mike—" Greg gives me a poke. "Forget about Ms. Salisbury. Look what's coming!"

On the other side of the playground, the mothers are showing up with their trays of cookies and cupcakes and pies. I reach into my pocket to make sure I still have the handful of change I emptied out of my bank this morning. All those goodies the mothers make for the P.T.A. sale are not only yummy, they're cheap.

The bell rings for us to go to our homerooms. I try to put Ms. Salisbury and the school psychologist and everything else out of my mind, so I can concentrate on deciding what I'm going to eat.

Then I get a great idea. I'm going to buy a whole pie—all for myself! Now all I have to decide is what kind.

When it's time for the Fiesta, everybody reports out on the playground, which is now decorated like a party with balloons and piñatas and paper streamers. All the tables that

Greg and I helped set up have bright paper tablecloths on them, and the mothers are setting out the food.

I wish the dancing part was over, so I could get the butterflies out of my stomach to make room for my pie.

All the visiting parents and little brothers and sisters are crowding onto the benches. I'm glad my mom is working and can't come. I'd be even more nervous about doing this dumb dance if she was watching me.

There's a platform set up with a microphone, and Mr. Mankowitz is getting ready to make a speech. I hope he's forgotten about my appointment with the school psychologist, but I don't think a principal ever forgets anything.

I don't have time to worry about that now—here comes Ms. Salisbury! Omigosh! She has on so many pink ruffles, I don't know how I'm going to get close enough to dance with her.

I can't even see her feet! How am I going to keep from stepping on them if I can't see them?

She claps her hands at us. "All right, everyone—find your partners and line up quietly. The dancing will begin as soon as Mr. Mankowitz finishes his welcome speech."

She takes my hand—*yuk*! "Come along, Michael, let's take our place." All the time Mr.

Mankowitz is speaking, I have to stand there holding hands with Ms. Salisbury! My palm gets so sweaty, it feels like we're glued together.

Finally, Mr. Mankowitz stops talking and the music for the square dance blares over the loudspeaker. "Here we go!" Ms. Salisbury sings out.

She pulls me along with her, and before I know it, I'm promenading out onto the middle of the playground hand in hand with my teacher, with practically the whole world watching. Mothers and fathers are nudging each other and pointing at us and smiling.

They're not laughing out loud because they have to be polite to Ms. Salisbury, but I can tell by their screwed-up faces that inside, they're laughing fit to kill. I feel my face getting redder than Greg's shirt.

Then, the worst thing in the world happens. My foot gets tangled up in one of Ms. Salisbury's pink ruffles. *Rrrr-rrrr-RIP!*

Every kid on the playground goggles at me and cracks up out of his mind, like it's the funniest thing he ever saw in his life. Even the grown-ups stop worrying about being polite and start laughing their heads off. The only one who isn't laughing is Ms. Salisbury.

And me.

... AND PIES

Ms. Salisbury's ruffle rips all the way off her dress and wraps around my ankle. Ron-the-Rat and Boom-Boom Bradley can hardly finish the dance, they're busting their guts laughing so hard. Man, it's the longest three and a half minutes of my life.

When the music finally stops, everybody claps but all I want to do is get away. Our group files off the playground, as the next bunch of dancers files on.

"That was lovely, everybody," says Ms. Salisbury, trying to unglue her hand from mine.

I unwind her ruffle off my ankle and hand it to her. "Sorry I tore your dress."

She pats my arm. "Don't fret about it,

Michael dear. You carried it off beautifully."

Ish! How gooey can you get! Why didn't she just get mad and yell at me? I hope nobody heard her.

Fat chance—with ol' eagle-ears Nicole around. As soon as Ms. Salisbury turns her back on us, Nicole gives me a toothy smile and mimics, "Don't fret about it, Michael *dear.* You carried it off *bee-yooo-tifully.*"

Ron and Boom-Boom bust their guts again.

"Get lost," I bark at Nicole, and the way her face crumples, you'd think *I* was picking on *her.* Go figure girls!

After all the dancing is finally over, Mr. Mankowitz speaks into the microphone again. "Thank you, boys and girls, for the entertainment. And now, it's time for refreshments."

About time! I'm sure ready to bury my troubles in a lemon meringue pie—that's the kind I've decided on—and I don't waste any time getting over to the food tables. But there's already a line about a mile and a half long.

Greg gets in line behind me. "You decided what you're going to get?"

"A lemon meringue pie—if there's still a whole one left by the time I get up there."

"You're going to eat a whole pie—all by yourself?"

"Why not?"

Greg grins. "Good idea. Wish I'd thought of it."

But the line isn't moving at all. "By the time we get up there," I mutter, "we'll be lucky if there's some cookie crumbs left."

"Right," Greg mutters back.

Ron swaggers up with Boom-Boom and Pete, the Basketball Killer. "What's holding things up?"

"Let's get this show on the road!"

"Move it, you guys!"

They try to shoulder in ahead of us, as if it's our fault the line isn't going anywhere. "Hey," I yell. "The end of the line is back there."

"The end of the line is for peasants." Pete plants himself in front of us with a look that dares us to do something about it.

Greg gives me a shrug, as if there really *isn't* anything we can do. But I feel this hard knot coming up out of my stomach into my throat, and I can't stop myself. I reach out and give Pete a shove.

It takes him by surprise and throws him off balance. He falls against the kids in line in front of him, and they turn around, mad. "Hey, watch it! Who d'you think you are?"

Pete jerks his thumb at me. "He pushed me."

"Yeah," Ron-the-Rat joins in. "It's *his* fault."

"Yeah? Well, give this right back to him!" All

the kids at the front end of the line shove back, and send all the kids at our end sprawling. Now everybody's mad and a big fight breaks out.

"Man, now look what you've started," Greg hollers at me, trying to keep out of the way of all the swinging arms and shoving bodies.

"What d'you mean—what *I* started?" I holler back over all the racket.

But I don't have time to argue—I'm too busy trying to keep out of the way, too. Guys are

wrassling together all over the place, and finally a couple of them knock over one of the food tables.

Some kids scoop up stuff to eat, but one guy starts using the cookies and cupcakes as hand grenades—and that *really* starts something!

Across the yard Mr. Mankowitz and a couple of the teachers are coming on the run. Then—

WOK! Something hits me in the face. I feel this goo smeared against my eyes and trickling off the end of my nose. I stick out my tongue and give a lick. Lemon meringue.

Just the kind I wanted. Lucky, huh?

Through a blur of meringue, I watch Mr. Mankowitz wade into the fray. The kids settle down fast.

"All right—who started this?" he demands.

"*He* did." Ron-the-Rat points at me.

"I did not." It's hard to protest with pie all over your face.

"Berger started the shoving," Pete puts in.

"These guys were trying to cut in line ahead of us," Greg tries to explain.

"That's no reason to start a fight," says Mr. Mankowitz. "Berger—go wash your face."

"Yes, sir."

"And you're to have that talk with Dr. Felix, first thing Monday morning."

"Yes, sir."

"The rest of you get to work and clean up this mess."

"Yes, Mr. Mankowitz," Pete and Boom-Boom chorus like a couple of Boy Scouts.

I head for the john and Greg tags along after me. "Dr. Felix, the school psychologist? What d'you have to talk to *him* for?"

"Mr. Mankowitz thinks I have a problem."

"*Do* you?"

"Yeah," I mutter. "I have to talk to Dr. Felix."

THE BIG SQUEAK

First thing Monday I head for Dr. Felix's office. But when I get to his door, I freeze. My stomach shrivels up and my arms and legs feel like they're made out of Tinkertoy sticks. I've never talked to a head doctor before.

I've only seen Dr. Felix once, standing in the hall one day with Mr. Mankowitz. He looked like Abraham Lincoln, about seven feet tall with a craggy face and short black beard.

I finally lift my Tinkertoy arm and knock on the door, and this soft deep voice says, "Come in."

I take a big breath, open the door and step inside. Dr. Felix is sitting at his desk, smiling this kind of sad smile. He looks even more like

Abraham Lincoln sitting down than he does standing up.

"Hello, Michael. Have a seat." I sink down in a big leather chair that feels as soft and deep

as Dr. Felix sounds. "Mr. Mankowitz tells me you have a problem. . . ."

"Not really. I mean . . . Well, things have just been getting kind of messed up lately, that's all."

"What kinds of things? Messed up how?" He sounds really interested.

I tell him about Nicole putting the Mouseketeer ears on my head in American History, and about Pete stealing my basketball and busting it, and those guys in the library getting me sent down. . . . I don't want to be a rat like Ron, though, so I'm careful not to mention any names.

Dr. Felix doesn't say anything. He just sits there, waiting for me to go on.

"Well . . . last Friday at the Fiesta . . . these guys came along and tried to crash into the food line ahead of me. I gave them a shove, and a big fight broke out. Mr. Mankowitz said it was all my fault, and somebody threw a lemon meringue pie in my face, besides."

"That's having things get kind of messed up, all right," Dr. Felix agrees. He leans across the desk and stares at me from under his black eyebrows. Suddenly, he yells in my face, "SO YOU'RE MAD AS HELL AND YOU'RE NOT GOING TO TAKE IT ANYMORE!"

I almost slide out of the big leather chair! Then I remember how I did the same thing to Mr. Mankowitz, and my face starts to burn.

"That was just a bumper sticker I saw once," I try to explain.

"But it's pretty much the way you're feeling—isn't it, Mike?"

"Yes, sir."

"Well, there's nothing wrong with yelling out your feelings once in a while." He smiles at me. "Only you should try to choose a better place than the principal's office."

"I know. I yelled it another time—in the hall when there was nobody around."

"That's a little better."

"Then . . . after that, I cried." When you're talking to somebody who looks like Abraham

Lincoln, you never know what you're going to tell him.

But Dr. Felix doesn't make a big thing of it. "Crying helps sometimes," he says. Then he asks me, "What else do you do—when things get 'kind of messed up'?"

I answer straight out. "Watch Mickey Mouse cartoons."

Dr. Felix leans back in his chair, smiling to himself as if he's thinking of a happy secret. "Good old Mickey. 'The squeak heard 'round the world.' "

He asks me which is my favorite Mickey cartoon of all (his is *The Sorcerer's Apprentice*), and have I ever seen the very first Mickey—*Steamboat Willie*?

"About twenty times," I tell him.

"Me too," says Dr. Felix. "Good old Mickey is a handy fellow to have around, isn't he?"

"Yes, sir."

"Especially when things get kind of messed up."

"Yes, sir."

Dr. Felix stands up, and from where I'm sitting deep down in the big leather chair, he looks about twelve feet tall. He smiles down on me. "Well, Mike—remember I'm here, too. If things get too messed up for you and Mickey to handle by yourselves. All right?"

65

"Yes, sir." I get up out of the chair. "Thanks, Dr. Felix." He shakes my hand, and I scoot out of his office and close the door behind me. It wasn't bad, but I'm glad it's over.

Greg is on the spot as usual, waiting out in the hall for me. "What happened?"

"Nothing. We just talked, that's all."

"What d'you talk about with a shrink?"

"You wouldn't believe me if I told you."

"Told me what?"

"Dr. Felix is a Mickey Mouse freak, too."

"You're kidding."

"I may even let him borrow my Mouseketeer ears sometime."

Greg grins. "How about that? Then I guess you don't have to worry, huh? Walt Disney is alive and well, and living in the hearts of the Good Guys."

"Yeah. Only—"

"Only what?"

"It's the Bad Guys who need him."

GOOD GUYS, BAD GUYS,
AND ME

It's getting to be the end of the school year, and that's all right with me. I'm sure ready for a vacation. Life gets a lot simpler in summer. You don't have to worry about D. S. Patterson and her stupid math drills. And you can run and yell all you want without getting sent down to some old principal's office.

And if I'm lucky, I might even make it from the middle of June to the middle of September without having anything at all to do with girls.

Maybe that's why, the last week of school, Nicole won't leave me alone. She even trails after me on my way home one day.

"Bug off, willya!"

"You're so mean, Mike Berger, you must eat worms for breakfast."

"That's right—and you better watch out or I'll upchuck 'em all over you."

Nicole's face gets that crumpled-up look again, as if *I* was picking on *her.*

I scowl at her. "Anyway, I'm *not* mean."

"Then why do you *act* mean?"

I guess I do, with Nicole. But who wouldn't? "Why d'you bug me all the time?" I want to know.

She stares at me with her Crayola eyes. "I thought somebody who liked Mickey Mouse the way you do would be . . . different."

"Different—*how*?"

Nicole shrugs. "Just not so mean—that's all." She tilts her chin in the air and whirls away from me, back down the street on her ballet toes, with her ponytail swishing behind her.

Good riddance! She doesn't know what she's talking about, so how am I supposed to figure it out?

I jog the rest of the way home, puffing out my cheeks and blowing out my breath in short spurts. It feels good.

I let myself in the front door and Jumbo in the back. He practically knocks me over, he's so glad to see me. I give his ears a good scratch.

"I'm sure glad you're not a weird little *girl* dog."

"Arf!" Jumbo agrees.

I fix us a snack and take it into my room to watch TV. There's a good war movie on. Ha! I guess Nicole would flip out if she knew I like to watch war movies, too. But you can't live on Mickey Mouse cartoons alone.

Anyway, what did she mean, she thought I was "different"? Did she think I was some kind of sissy or something?

"Well, I'm not—am I, Jumbo!"

"Arf!"

"But I'm not *mean*, either."

Jumbo reaches up to give me a sloppy lick on the cheek to prove it.

"Not as mean as Boom-Boom Bradley, anyway."

Only then I remember last Saturday when I saw Boom-Boom at the supermarket, wheeling a shopping cart around for some old lady—I don't know if it was his grandmother or who. He was sure embarrassed when he saw me, like I was going to spread the word around school that he wasn't such a big tough guy, after all.

And I guess maybe he isn't—not all the time. And if Nicole says I'm mean, maybe *I'm* not always the Good Guy I thought I was. I'm going to have to think about that!

The picture comes on the TV screen, and Jumbo and I stretch out on my bed to watch.

Right away, it starts with a big noisy battle. Jumbo jumps down off the bed and crawls under it.

"Don't worry, Jumbo. The Good Guys'll win. They always do." On TV, anyway.

Now that I think about it, maybe that's why there's no justice in this world, like my mom says. I mean—you can't always *tell* who's a Good Guy and who's a Bad Guy. Maybe even Walt Disney couldn't do anything about *that*.

All the same—I'm sure glad he invented Mickey Mouse.